Bear's Busy Family
La famille active de l'Ours

Stella Blackstone
Debbie Harter

Barefoot Books
step inside a story

Smell the bread
my grandma bakes.

Sens le pain
que ma grande-mère fait.

**Touch the bowls
my grandpa makes.**

Touche les bols
que mon grand-père fabrique.

Taste the fish
my uncle brings.

Goûte le poisson
que mon oncle apporte.

Hear the songs
my auntie sings.

Écoute les chansons
que ma tante chante.

**See the dress
my mama sews.**

Regarde la robe
que ma maman coud.

Smell the flowers
my papa grows.

Sens les fleurs
que mon papa fait pousser.

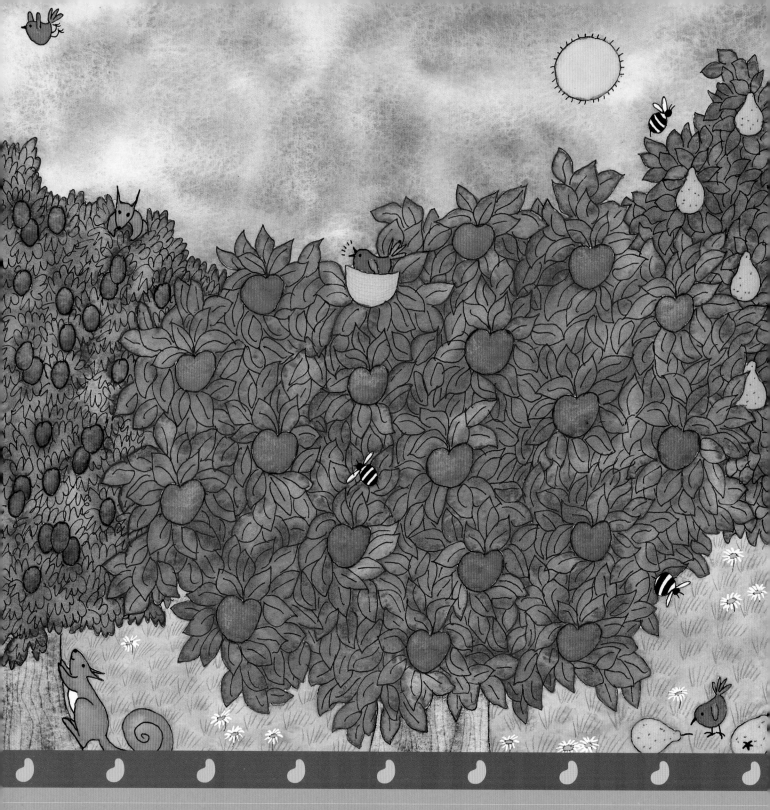

Touch the plums
my sister picks.

Touche les prunes
que ma sœur cueille.

Taste the bowl
my brother licks.

Goûte le bol
que mon frère lèche.

**Hear the drums
my cousins play.**

Écoute les tambours
que mes cousins jouent.

See the feast for baby's birthday!

Regarde la fête pour l'anniversaire de bébé!

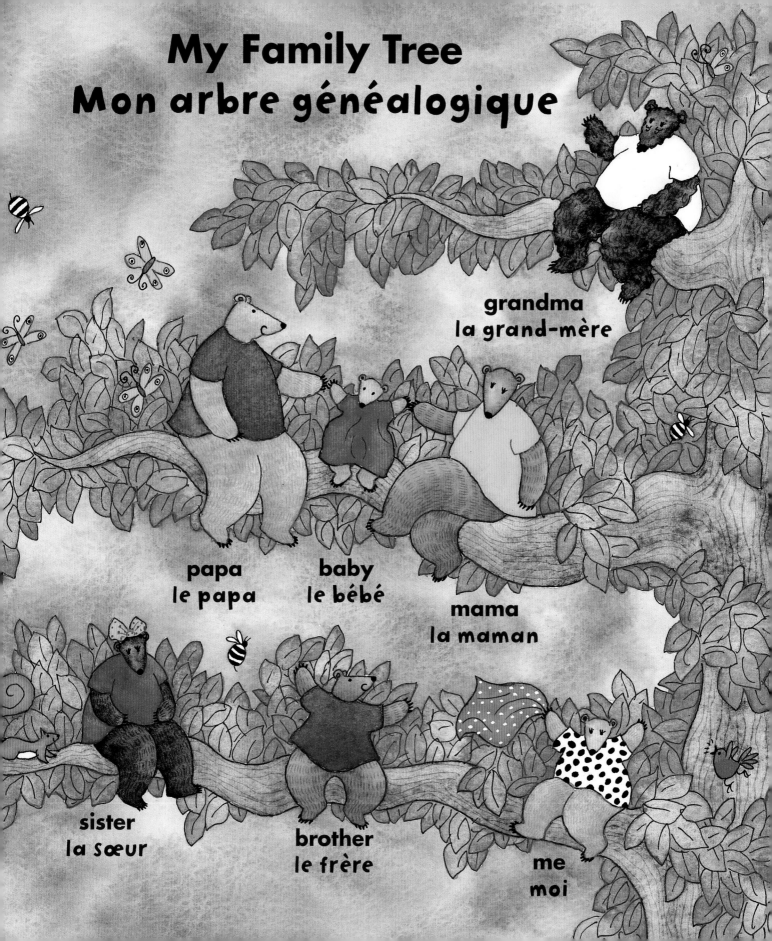

My Family Tree
Mon arbre généalogique

grandma
la grand-mère

papa
le papa

baby
le bébé

mama
la maman

sister
la sœur

brother
le frère

me
moi

grandpa
le grand-père

uncle
l'oncle

aunt
la tante

cousins
les cousins

Vocabulary / *Vocabulaire*

Hello. – *Bonjour.*

Good-bye. – *Au revoir.*

Yes. – *Oui.*

No. – *Non.*

Please? – *S'il vous plaît?*

Thank you. – *Merci.*

Pardon me. – *Excuse-moi.*

I'm sorry. – *Je suis désolé.*

How are you? – *Ça va?*

I'm fine, thank you. – *Ça va bien, merci.*

Barefoot Books
294 Banbury Road
Oxford, OX2 7ED

Barefoot Books
2067 Massachusetts Ave
Cambridge, MA 02140

Text copyright © 1999 by Stella Blackstone
Illustrations copyright © 1999 by Debbie Harter
The moral rights of Stella Blackstone and Debbie Harter have been asserted

First published in Great Britain by Barefoot Books, Ltd
and in the United States of America by Barefoot Books, Inc in 1999
This bilingual French edition first published in 2012
All rights reserved

Graphic design by Tom Grzelinski, Bath and Louise Millar, London
Reproduction by Grafiscan, Verona
Printed in China on 100% acid-free paper
This book was typeset in Futura and Sloppy
The illustrations were prepared in watercolor, pen and ink, and crayon

ISBN 978-1-84686-772-9

British Cataloguing-in-Publication Data:
a catalogue record for this book is available from the British Library

Library of Congress Cataloging-in-Publication Data
is available upon request

Translator: Eleanor Loftie

1 3 5 7 9 8 6 4 2